1

The Embalmer

By Rayne Havok

Rights

This is a work of fiction, if you find any similarities what- so- ever they are coincidental.

No part of this book may be copied or reproduced without prior authorization from the author.

For you, my obsession.

Summary

Sadie is tempted by a body in the funeral home. She can't help herself, her curiosity is too strong. The depraved and obscene thoughts won't disappear, and with nothing holding her back, she succumbs to her sick desires.

Warning

I'm told this book should have a warning.

Because these things are always in my head and on my mind, I don't always consider them to be over- the- top. To some it may be run- of- the mill and to others it may be too much.

If you feel like you may have issues reading 'extreme' stories please do not bother with this one, you may be offended.

I do not condone any of this shit in real life, please remember this is a work of fiction and as always do not try this at home.

one

The thin white sheet is tenting. I can't keep my eyes off of it.

There is a common misconception that when men die, they get an erection, and unless you are face down with the blood pooling in that direction, it's simply untrue.

That guy, however, is sporting a huge erection. Cause of death, heart attack. He's not the body I'm working on right now, he is next in line, though.

James has been working on the same old man for over an hour, they're always a challenge, their faces sag and it's hard to make them look life- like in order for their families to recognize them. He's an expert though, and I have every confidence that he will do an excellent job. His back is to me, and I'm glad, I definitely can't get caught eyeballing the dead dudes junk.

I can't seem to get over how big it is, I keep catching myself losing track of what I'm doing and fantasizing about what might be under there.

I've honestly never given any other body more than a cursory look, nothing but business for the greying and flaccid ones. But this man, whose sheet is tucked under the chiseled chin of a god, has me curious. The sheet can't hide how sculpted his body is, I can tell he is in perfect shape, I can't imagine the reason for the heart attack unless it was genetic. Sad, really, seems like such a waste.

I catch myself breathing heavy, and when James asks me if I'm ok, I drag my tongue across my dry lips and swallow hard, trying to recoup the semblance of normalcy. Then tell him I'm fine, that I have a headache and I need a moment.

I take a cigarette from my pack and head up the stairs to the main floor of the house and as far away from the converted basement as I can get right now. I light it before I'm outside and I pull the drag deep into my lungs before blowing it out, along with the thoughts that really shouldn't be there anyway.

What the fuck is wrong with you?

I cannot get over how affected I am by this whole thing. I've never been so interested in something like this before, sure there have been times where curiosity had gotten the better of me and maybe I wondered. But this, this is not wondering, this is fantasizing– this is lust.

I'm soaked between my legs, the heat is practically radiating throughout my core, even while standing outside on a brisk day without my coat, which I left in my hasty getaway, I'm hot.

I take another long pull and slowly let the smoke out, expelling even more air than needed, in hopes that I can get that sheet and all the implications hiding under it out from under my skin.

I flick the butt near the ashtray, not giving it too much of an effort, and then head back down the stairs.

James is grabbing the keys to the transport van and I ask him 'what's up?'

"Twenty something female, gunshot wound."

I look at the taboo man lying on the table, and before I can stop myself I say, "I can get her, you could take care of this one."

He gives me a strange look. I never volunteer for transport. He brushes my offer to the side and grabs his jacket.

"I'll be back as soon as I can."

"Thanks," I say back, hoping I haven't confused him too much.

I wait until the door closes before returning to the forty- two year old suicide on my table, I just have to finish her neck, she hung herself and did quite a bit of damage in the process.

I'm annoyed that I'm not done already, I should have been able to knock this one out quickly and moved on to the next, except that's what I'm procrastinating. I can't imagine putting my hands on him in any capacity and not touching him inappropriately. Wrapping my fingers around that big cock I see, barely hiding under there.

I can't keep my feet from walking forward, my head keeps telling them to stop, but they hear the half- heartedness behind the pleas. I need to see what's under there.

Just a peak to quench the curiosity. Then I can get the fuck back to work.

I take that peek, but I don't cover him back up like I thought I would, instead I'm stuck staring. He must have had some sort of augmentation done on it. That would explain the rigidity and the slight scar I see around the circumference about midway up his thick shaft.

I can't stop my shaking hand from reaching out. My mind is foggy with confusion and lust. I know I want this, but I don't *want* to want this. I don't want to feel the need, the desire to do this, to touch him. I want to remain the normal girl, with normal thoughts. I want to think this is repulsive, but I can't.

The smoothness of his cock sends a thrill across my body. I've never touched a corpse with anything other than professional intentions. Never given it a single thought.

This man, for some reason, has me twisted inside, conflicted, and fucking *horny*.

The excitement inside of me is overflowing; I can't stop myself from stroking him. He can't feel it, so I know it's only for my own sake. I must want to feel him like this, sliding inside my fisted hand. Slowly, I glide my hand from base to tip, squeezing hard at the tip, then back down.

I can feel the rhythm inside my core, images of him inside of me, accepting his full length deeply. Then the thoughts of him lying here while I do it spring into my mind. I like that he's here on the gurney, that he can't say anything, that he would be used for my pleasure alone. I hold myself back but let my imagination run away, let it go toward what it's craving.

It takes me to the very depths of the disgusting thoughts that I'm only now realizing I have inside me. I have a very healthy and active sex life, but I can say with a hundred percent certainty, that I've not been this wet for any other man, or reason, in my life. I let go of his shaft only long enough to grab his chart, I don't know what I'm looking for until I find it. His STD results. They'd done a swab of it and the results are negative.

I can't wrap my head around why I even care. What does that mean? Is this feeling right now so strong that I know I'm going to do something about it? Does it mean I want to?

Before I can answer any of those questions, the double doors swing open and James pulls the gurney in through the door. Luckily, his back is to me and I have time to right the sheet. I can't believe how distracted I let myself become, how overwhelming this pull is for me that I'd almost lost everything for it. My god, that would have been awful.

"Hey, James," is all I can say, and it probably shouldn't have been said in the first place, I never welcome him back.

He must realize it too, because he looks at me with his brows raised. "You need something, Sadie?"

"Nope… just this damn headache again."

"I think it must be the chemicals today."

I notice, then, that his face is flush and looks a little green. "What's going on with you?"

"I think I've got a cold coming on, can't get over this nausea thing." I see it then, just how bad he looks, and it makes me feel horrible for him.

"We could just put her in the fridge and you could take off. I'll get these two sorted out," I offer.

His face looks like he'll take me up on it, but he says he'll stay.

"Really, don't worry about it. I need to finish with the suicide anyway. I'll just tuck these ones away, we'll get to them tomorrow. You look like shit. I can take an aspirin for mine. You need bedrest, plus, you're probably contagious, and I don't want to catch that shit." It comes out a little harder than I intend, but seriously... gross.

"Yea, that might be for the best." He drags her body to the fridge and slides it inside.

"I'll get these two." I say a little too quickly, hopefully his ailment is keeping him a little slower mentally than normal, and not as keen to notice how weird I'm acting.

He doesn't seem to notice my oddities and I'm grateful for it.

I watch, without moving an inch, out of fear alone, as he gathers his things and heads to the door.

Relief floods when I realize I'm alone. I can hardly think straight since almost being caught in the act of defiling the corpse.

I do the only thing I can do right now, while holding tightly to my rational self. I put this fucker in the fridge, shoving the door hard to latch it. Then I finish with the woman who should have been done already and joining him, but still she needs my attention. Her funeral is tomorrow, and I have to get her looking her best for it.

I think of anything I can to keep my mind free of him and it works. I'm able to nearly forget about him in the cooler. And by the time the woman looks as near perfect as she's going to get, he is a distant memory.

Almost.

I do have to jog up the stairs to fight a bit of curiosity creeping back in. But, once I'm upstairs, I am able to eat and watch some television before tucking in to bed for the night.

two

I'm having trouble sleeping, obviously my subconscious is not able to calm down from all the excitement. As soon as my eyes are open, my thoughts are on that man downstairs. Maybe it's living in such close proximity to him. Maybe it's my morbid fascination with him, for some reason I cannot understand, he has me trapped inside a loop of curiosity.

As I lay in bed, I try very hard to focus on the realization of what would happen if I gave in to my thoughts, if I stoked them with a bit more reality. If I followed, what my legs want me to do right now, and walked down the stairs to him, peacefully lying there on the slab of frigid metal. What would it take from me if I did that? What would be the consequences to my soul?

I can hardly think. The rambling and scrambled thoughts have been obscured by the picture my head has created of him down there, completely naked beneath the thin sheet, his thick muscles hardened by physical activity and a gorgeous face to boot.

Fuck.

I can't stay here, I can't just pretend like I am able to accomplish that. I know I don't morally find anything wrong with what

I have in my mind. It is a crime, but a victimless one. Honestly, if I think about it, I know that I don't abide by all of societies laws, I don't let a red light stop me if no one is around, I don't let the grapes eaten in the grocery store bog me down with guilt.

I shouldn't let this weigh on me, shouldn't let what society thinks is appropriate define what I think is nothing more than getting off. No matter what, I'm the only one who has to live with this, and I am willing. For fucks sake, the guy is dead. What does he care?

I let my feet take me down the winding staircase and around the corner to flip the light switch, the fluorescent bulbs flicker until they charge and brighten the room.

My slippers drag on the floor, making the only noise in the silent room. It is always so quiet down here after hours. Not that it has the hustle and bustle during operating hours, but it's eerie in here at night.

I go to the drawer that holds my heart attack guy with the boner and pull on the door, then slide the drawer out. I catch myself looking around the room, subconsciously aware that what I'm about to do is wrong, but still wanting to do it. Almost needing to do it, the compulsion is driving me mad.

I move the sheet slowly down his body, uncovering his hairy chest. He has the light shade of grey that people have once they're dead, it doesn't even phase me. I don't pause, I continue moving down his body. Standing next to him, I lean over the bottom drawer and take his cock in my hand again. This time I intend to do something other than just groping. There is no stopping me now.

I lift up my long shirt over my head and straddle the man, resting my ass on his thighs. The cool feel of his body sends a shiver up my spine. The rush of cold hits me fast, he's hard underneath me.

I put my hands on him and feel the tightness of his chest. I close my eyes and feel him, touch everywhere. Run my fingers across his body and down to the meaty cock that interrupted my sleep, then I raise up to hover over it, rubbing it against my clit. I hiss. The feel of it against my hotness is a sensation I will never forget. I thought it might cool me down, but it does not, the drastic temperature change exhilarates me.

I let it enter me slowly, gingerly lowering myself down on it. It does the same thing to my insides– cools them, but only in temperature, nothing can take this from the top of my hot and naughty list.

Moving with purpose, I let myself experience every inch of this man's big cock. I feel the fullness of him and am compelled to move faster, running my hand down my chest, across my trembling stomach, until I find the little nub that's begging to be touched, then rub circles around it.

My breathing, the sound I can't hold in when being fucked, and the tiny moans that escape me interrupt the quiet room. I keep one hand on him for balance as I quicken the pace. I get lost with him inside of me, the feel of my orgasm creeps in and I rub harder– fuck harder– deeper than I've ever been reached.

I come hard and loud, then fuck myself frantically on top of him. So frantic, in fact, that I don't hear the noise. The noise that I should have heard, that would not have happened if I wasn't preoccupied with this man. If I could have just kept my wits about me, I would have remembered to lock the lower entrance doors to the room.

But, instead, they swing wide open. The heavy door hits the wall and it only slightly alarms me. I don't stop, I can't, not until the voice comes. The voice that doesn't belong to James, but instead a stranger.

"Holy fuck!" says the voice, which I match to the man as soon as my eyes open. He has a phone in his hand, and it's pointed right at me.

I'm at a loss for what to do. I stumble off the slab, to the floor, on my hands and knees.

I'd be embarrassed by that if I weren't mortified from being caught fucking a dead body.

My face is red, the heat of shame crept up my neck, I'm flushed. I can't get to my feet, I can't do anything but bury my face on the cold cement floor.

I hardly realize that I should be concerned about the three men standing in front of me. It dawns on me that I shouldn't be thinking of my embarrassment, instead, I should be pissed, or at the very least, I should be scared.

They are huge men. Three. Huge. Men.

I get to my feet with very little grace, but it's done now, and I square my shoulders and meet their faces. Each one of them.

The first is tallest and thinnest, but that doesn't mean he is not intimidating.

He is.

The second is slightly shorter, thick, in the way that you know he has muscles, but they're hiding underneath a layer of fat. He's glaring at me.

I move quickly to the last, he's tall and muscular, covered in tattoos up to his neck. Bright and colorful. His hair is short, making it easier to see them all. He has a smile on his face– more of a smirk, really, watching me through the lens of his phone.

"Nice to meet you," he says, finally meeting my eyes.

The accent is thick, I can't place it. I'm not good at pinpointing regions, if it weren't so apparent I might not have even noticed it.

"Shut up, Rhys," the glaring fat man says.

"Just being polite," he says back at him without looking away from me.

The blush comes back, this time it's from the thoughts that just came into my head of him whispering into my ear, telling me such dirty things with that voice. It's low and gravely, and coupled with the accent, sends me over the top.

I swallow hard and avert my eyes. I don't miss the huge grin that crosses his face before I can get away. My mouth dries until it feels like a desert, making me anxious. I have to be able to speak to these men. And hopefully that's all they'll be doing to me tonight.

"You get a lady in here tonight?" the thin one asks.

"Uhhh." I can't remember anything at this point, I can't recall something to help him.

"She'd be blonde, big tits— she got shot." The fat man cuts off his friend, obviously taking the lead.

I gather my thoughts and realize, they're looking for the lady James brought in earlier. I didn't get a good look at her but I know she is blonde. I try and rack my brain for the number of the cubby we put her in.

They look impatient. I get nervous. I don't do well under pressure. That's why I work with dead people. It has always promised little to no social interactions. But, I guess, if you start fucking them, bad things happen. I just never imagined it would be thugs showing up in the middle of the night looking for a corpse.

I point to the door they should open to find her. Rhys walks over and pulls on it. Luckily, I was right; there she is, covered with a sheet, completely untouched by us. He pulls the sheet off her and lets it fall to the floor.

"Give me the shit you found in her," the fat leader says.

I forgo the on- the- tip- of- my- tongue sarcastic remark and keep my composure.

"We haven't done anything to her, yet," I say.

"Really? Why is she all cut up then?" Rhys says in his sexy accented way.

I can't help it, it flusters me and makes me so fucking hot. He has one of those rolling r's.

"Um," I take a deep breath. "She had an autopsy done, we didn't embalm her yet." I hope it sounds as strong as I planned, I'm practically swooning. I have always had a thing for accents. The way I imagine his tongue would feel on me, using it to give me exactly what I want. Buried between my legs– eating me– fucking me with the very thing that is making me wet right now.

"So, it should still be in here, the guy at the hospital said they hadn't found anything," Rhys says to me.

"I don't know what you're looking for. I haven't seen her before."

"She had drugs in her tits when she died. We need to get them back." He looks at me expectantly.

"I don't want any part of this," I say.

"Listen, bitch, you are a part of this. And if you want to walk away right now, I'm sure I could show a few of the right fucking people that you were caught fucking Mr. Big Cock over there when we walked in," the fat boss says.

He's angry and I don't try and tell him he would implicate himself in some pretty bad things if he were to do that.

"Calm the fuck down, Leo," Rhys tells him, putting his phone in his back pocket. As if I needed one more reason for him to be attractive. Coming to a lady's rescue, even when you are a strong female, is always nice. It does get him a glare from the leader, Leo.

Knowing their names worries me; I hope they don't think they need to kill me.

Leo takes over the conversation, but does so with a little less hatred spewing remarks. "I need you to get our shit out of her titties."

I'm confused as to how it may have been missed during autopsy. I mean, things are overlooked, but implants are usually found pretty easily, without even looking for them.

I walk over to see if it was in this case. I feel around her chest and can easily confirm she's got her implants still inside. Reaching for a scalpel I cut across the stitches put there by a lazy M.E.– or assistant, I'd say, by the lack of precision.

I fold back the skin and see that the implants are intact and inside. I remove the first, after putting a glove on, and hand it over to the thin man, whose hand is reaching for it.

I don't have too much time with it, but I can confirm the implant is full of drugs, a black substance in tiny bags within the implant sack– whatever that might be, I have no idea.

"And the other," Leo says, impatiently.

I quickly go after the other one, handing it over swiftly. The thin guy holds one in each hand, not really knowing what to do with them. It might look funny, if I weren't so fucked right now.

"Ok," I say, more to fill the silence.

"Let's go, Leo," Rhys says, turning his back to me, effectively blocking me from seeing the intense conversation they're having with each other using only their eyes.

"Fine, but if she gets even a *little* messy, she's fuckin' done. And I know you know what I mean by *done*," Leo says to Rhys, before turning to the thin guy and saying, "Let's go."

They leave me alone with Rhys to explain how shit is going to go, assuming I'm willing to comply. Although, if I'm not, I am certain he is supposed to kill me. I can see it in his eyes. There's a hint of pleading in them. I can't hold his gaze, I look down at his colorful arms instead. Then down to his thick fingers, then over a few inches to his crotch.

Damn it.

This man has seriously affected me; something about him, I couldn't name it if I tried, has gotten to me and wrapped itself around my insides.

"Listen, beautiful lady, I need you to behave."

"Ok," I say, but I don't know if he is referring to me looking at his crotch or if he means the task at hand. The thing they talked about without words.

"Thanks for such a nice compliment, by the way." He brings his eyes to the front of his pants and I know he did catch me.

I wish I didn't blush every fucking time I heard him speak. I wish he didn't have this thing that captivated me. I'm completely lost in whatever this attraction I have to him.

The way he speaks, the simple words, whatever they are, completely hypnotize me. The cadence of his accent, and the ease in which he forms his words, is wrapping around my head and swirling inside my tummy.

Standing here fully naked, and literally caught with a dead guy inside of me, doesn't stop my nipples from exposing my state of complete arousal. I can feel my lust trickling down the inside of my clenched thighs. Somehow it is not as awkward as it clearly should be. He has this ease about him, some sort of swagger that screams to me and makes all my inhibitions melt away.

"I'm sure you know, that Leo will follow through with what he said. He will leak the video."

I can only shake my head; my voice wouldn't work even if I tried.

"You heard Leo, he's ok with you, so long as you can help us out with a few things. The people we have dealings with that may end up going south," he looks at me poignantly. "We need you to help with those. You can do that, right?"

I don't know what the fuck I can do for them. I have James here most days and I can't necessarily have a stream of people coming and going as they please without raising suspicion. But I tell him yes. I know I don't want to fuck with these men, I don't want to end up dead, and they look exactly the type to do something like that if I can't be useful.

"Ok, so for now, you just hold tight and wait, I can't say when we may need you."

"How are you going to let me know you need my help? I have a partner that will start asking questions and possibly get suspicious if he sees people like you hanging around."

"People like me?" he has a flirty smirk on his face. "What are people like *me*?"

"I don't know, thugs?" I regret it the second it's out of my mouth, I really shouldn't be tempting fate, I should be being on my best behavior, considering who I'm in front of.

"Little lady, I suggest you watch your mouth when we are not alone, I know Leo and Thomas wouldn't like hearing that."

I can hear the seriousness in his voice, which is even hotter when he's laying down the law and being stern. "Ok," I say. I can hardly contain the shiver I feel cover my body.

I can see he is aware of the effect he has on me, his eyes follow the length of my body, and the scrutiny arouses me. "Anyway," he shakes his head and refocuses on my eyes. "We can be discreet, so long as you can be helpful. I'll make sure the others know that we'd have to wait for after hours to do business."

"Thank you." I don't know why it sounds like he's conceding, I wonder what it would be like for me here if he weren't being so reasonable– if I could even use that word in this context.

"I'll take a key for the doors here."

"Uh… I think you can just ring the bell." I don't want them down here fishing around in things while I'm upstairs sleeping, or if James shows up earlier than me, I can't have him find things.

"That won't do. Key. Now."

Well, since he's using his stern voice again, I really can't deny him. I take the spare from the ring by the door and put it inside his waiting hand. "You need to put whoever it is in the drawer right here." I point to the one that we never use, center row, last box. It has a sticky roller that makes it a pain in the ass to pull out.

"Got it." He's all business now, the spark of flirtation is gone. It makes me want to cover up more than ever. I finally *feel* naked.

"See you later, love," he says, then turns to go.

I wait until the heavy door closes completely before I move. The first thing I do is lock it.

three

The next few days I have some of the most vivid dreams of Rhys. I wake covered in cold sweats of arousal. Obsession– if I'm actually honest with myself. His voice pulls me awake, even though he's not here, I hear him perfectly inside my brain.

The days pass, and I find nothing in the drawer, I'm jittery and jumpy at every sound. James takes notice right away. I didn't have an answer for the reason, so our relationship is strained. I'm sure he is thinking it's something he has done. But how can I explain the real reason for the distance and weird behavior? I can't.

I'm almost able to pretend that the night never happened, when I hear the lock click. I'm alone, and cleaning everything for the next day, when the doors swing open. The three men file inside, Thomas, the tall, thin one, carrying a body.

Fuck.

"Nice to see you in something other than your birthday suit," Leo says.

"Not really," Rhys says under his breath. That gets him a look of disapproval from Leo.

He shrugs it off. "What? She's hot."

"Anyway… we got something for you." He nods to Thomas, who then brings the body forward. I point to the table and he sets the man down. Both Thomas and the body are covered in blood.

"What am I supposed to do with him? You got something inside of him too?"

"No, we need you to get rid of him," Rhys says.

I look up at him, a better place to focus my attention anyway. "Why?" I regret the question right away, I shouldn't ask these things that I know could be detrimental to my health, but I've never been in a situation where I had to watch myself so closely. "I'm sorry. I don't need to know that," I say to no one in particular.

Leo moves forward, putting himself close enough that I could touch him. "Don't push me, bitch. You will not like what I do to people taking an interest in what I do."

I press my lips together and nod at him, trying my hardest not to cower. I hate being called a bitch simply for my gender, but I let it go. I mean, what else am I supposed to do?

"So, you want me to make the body disappear. Is that it?"

"Yes."

"In the chamber? You want me to cremate him?" I hope that's what he's asking, I can't imagine what else he wants me to do. Burying him is out of the question, but I could easily run the incinerator if he wanted me to.

"You got it. No trace, fast and easy."

"Alright." Relief takes the weight from my shoulders and I relax. If this is all they want from me, I could be all right. I do it all day anyway.

They stand around, instead of leaving as I thought they would.

Rhys walks over and helps me lift the man from the table. "Leo has some trust issues," he whispers into my ear. I cannot imagine a better way to get through this than him whispering directions to me.

In a way, I'm kind of glad this is all happening. As fucked up as it seems, and all things considered, it hasn't been as bad as it could be. Disposing of a few bodies here and there isn't awful. I do it on a daily basis for work, and as we've recently learned, my morals are not that of an upstanding citizen.

After closing the door on the oven, Rhys comes to stand right behind me; he puts his hands on my shoulders then leans in close to whisper in my ear, "it will get easier." The t's and s fall softly from his lips onto the hair of my neck, sending electricity through my skin before the r rolls its way into my ear, goosebumps erupt along my spine.

I don't know if he's picking up on some other sort of dilemma I'm having and assigning the agitation to this ordeal, but I do have to say, it's nice that he notices these things.

He squeezes my shoulders a couple times, digging deep into the muscles, and if we were alone, I'd turn right now and put my mouth on his. Instead, I struggle to restrain the moan that is threatening to escape, and then I take a step away before it's impossible.

He doesn't move away, so I come face to face with him when I turn, his eyes burn right into mine. I can feel his thoughts; feel everything they're saying to me. He's so reassuring in them, without words, his beautiful blue eyes tell me he will keep me safe, and I trust that he will.

The only thing that can take my eyes from his is what he does next. I catch a glimpse of his pink tongue, the same tongue that has become my obsession, licking his full bottom lip, leaving behind wetness that I can't help but want to taste.

My own comes out on a subconscious adventure and I bite my lip to keep from saying anything about it, balling my hands into fists at my side to keep from touching him. The pain in my lip hits me seconds later, and I let it go before I draw blood.

The whole thing only takes a minute, at the most, but it feels like so much has happened. So many tiny and intricate things transpired in that time that I feel overwhelmed. The feelings that I can't accept, because it makes me crazy to think that love at first sight might exist. And that

I'm staring at it in the face. It scares me to no end. But I can't help myself, I know that this is real, I know that what I feel is something otherworldly. Something that happens when two people have the same need, that someone could pick up on that and meet it. I can't help but feel this man is my need, and only he will do to fill it.

He finally steps back; I see the miniscule tick of regret on his face. I know he was where I was mentally, thinking all the same things. He also knows that now is not the time, so he takes himself out of it.

"Alright, we done here?" he asks Leo.

"Yep, looks like the lady is useful after all, good call, Rhys." Then he turns to me. "Be seeing you, little lady."

The two men leave ahead of Rhys, who I think will say something to me in confidence, but he doesn't. He just looks into my hungry eyes and does his rendition of the sexiest smile I've ever seen. It takes the breath from my lungs, stirs up the little sleeping butterflies in my stomach and fucks my mind into a complete mess.

Then he leaves, and I'm feeling the loss instantly, the room is empty, and feels cold without him in it. I take a deep breath before I pass out and crumble to the floor. My legs won't work to move, so I stay planted, staring at the door. Eventually, I find the strength to tame the tremors so I can leave.

Knowing I'll just lie in bed, shuffling through the thoughts, the what- ifs, and possibilities of him. His words, however few, replaying in my head, hearing all the meaning behind the limited words we can say in those brief moments. I am able to survive this whole ordeal only because of those times I get to spend near him.

four

I do just as I assume, and lie awake, alone and yet somehow not. He's right here with me even if it is only in thought. Sleep is hard to chase down, and when I finally fall, it is at the very tip, restless and fidgety. I wake with the sun, much earlier than I like, but what I have become accustomed to since meeting Rhys.

I lie in my bed; full minutes pass, as I try to rid my thoughts of him. I can't help but bring my hand between my legs, swollen and aching. I rub that pesky little nub until I come, and still, I find no relief. Frustrated and unsatisfied, I leave the bed in a pissed off mood.

I get ready to start the day, I'd be early going downstairs to work, but I have nothing else to put my focus into, so I get ready and rush downstairs to drown in routine.

It's dark until I turn the light on, I pull open the cadaver drawer and get to work immediately on the man I left here last night. His funeral is this evening and I shouldn't have put him off this long, but I can hardly focus on what needs to be done.

He only needs a few touch ups, he's relatively young and there was no trauma to his exterior. I get lost in the particulars of my job, humming to the music that fills the air.

I hear the door open and look up a moment later, expecting to see James, but am confronted by the three men I have grown to both love and hate.

"You do know that it's business hours," I say to the group, a little harsher than is smart.

"Got a job, can't wait around all day for you to be available," Leo, ever the friendly guy, says.

"Then, by all fucking means, what can I do to serve you?" I put my hand on my hip to emphasize my irritation. It's still early, and I'm not really expecting James, but the deal was agreed upon and I can't let them get away without, at the very least, letting them know I'm annoyed.

It's the fucking principle.

"Got one of our own, he needs to be looked after," Rhys chimes in, and simply hearing that accented voice calms everything inside of me.

"K, bring him in." I roll my eyes, more at myself, than anyone else. This man truly could ask me for anything at this point and I'd drop everything for him to make him happy.

Leo and Thomas leave together, I assume to do what I said, and Rhys comes toward me. The butterflies are back, the freefalling starts, and I try and hold myself upright.

"Thank you, he means a lot to us, wouldn't want anyone else to handle this," he says, reaching out and tucking a stray hair behind my ear. The brief touch warms my skin and flushes my face. I suck my lip into my mouth, this time I don't bite down, this time I'm only trying to stop myself from saying something stupid.

My eyes tick across his face, from the top of his forehead down, so I can remember every detail, memorize it for later, when I can close them and recall every tiny nuance of him. The tiny scar across his eyebrow, the light freckles that dot the bridge of his nose, which has a slight bump on the bridge, I can't tell if it's from a break or just how it's always been. I don't miss a single thing, though.

I feel compelled to ask him, but I don't, instead, I let my eyes wander lower. The neck of his wife- beater is low enough to see the spatter of hair that would be hidden in another type of shirt. There are tons of women that love a smooth and hairless chest; I however, have never been one.

I catch all the intricate detail of his artwork and find a small coin shaped scar under one of them, slightly raised.

"What's that from?" I ask, meeting his eyes that were busy watching me during my inspection.

"Had a bad step dad who used me like an ashtray for his cigars. It's not the only one down there."

He doesn't sound like it traumatized him, it does, however, sound like it still pisses him off.

"Oh." It's the only thing I can get out before the doors slam open. I startle and scramble away like I'd been caught doing something awful.

I look over to him when I hear the chuckle that tells me I'm being ridiculous. I can't help but smile back at him.

"Put him in the cooler," I tell the men, who look at me for direction.

I see Leo may have a problem with the instruction and I tell him, "I can't do anything with him right now, James will be here soon and I can't explain to him why the incinerator is on when we have no scheduled cremations today."

"Fine," Leo concedes, "but I want it done tonight, if I find out you fucked off and didn't, you'll fucking regret it."

"I got it. Not my first time." I hold his stare until he breaks it on his end. Following my lead to the cooler, I open the door and slide out the metal table for them. They get him situated and I can't help but notice the resemblance to Rhys. They both have dark hair and a softer looking face, some might call it a baby face, but for the dotting of hair that looks as though they've missed a few days of shaving.

I look over to Rhys, checking to see if there is a familial resemblance, or if it is just a coincidence. The look on his face is not that of someone who has lost anyone other than a friend. So I feel better for him– guessing I'm right in my assumption.

I shut the door, and just in time. I hear the roar of James's truck. It's a too- big thing that makes all sorts of unnecessary noise. I'm grateful for it now, and rush them up the stairs, telling them, that unless they want to get caught in here and ruin a good thing, they'll follow me. I hear nothing but footsteps from them as they rush up behind me.

I unlock the door and close it behind us all, just as I hear James downstairs, slamming the door shut.

I walk them straight to the front door, holding it open expectantly. The men take their leave and I have a rush of relief as they don't argue or take liberties with my house. It's one thing for them to be in the basement, a completely different thing when invited into my home, where they may now feel is open to them.

I watch Rhys walk away, he doesn't turn and I don't really expect him to. The sure way he carries himself is fucking beautiful, he has a swagger that can only come from confidence. His low hung jeans hanging on by the roundedness of his ass, it is truly hypnotic. I take a shaky breath and head downstairs when I no longer have my eye candy to look at.

"You get here early?" James asks.

"Yea, couldn't sleep, I am about finished with number eight though, so he'll be ready for tonight." I head in that direction now, keeping my head down and eyes averted, jumping right back in where I left off. A few finishing touches, and I'm done in no time.

We have gotten back into our work-flow again, letting the awkwardness go, working together nicely. The day passes quickly and James heads out when he is done with his last job, leaving me to finish with mine, and what I almost forgot– the body in the cooler. I can't believe I hadn't given it another thought. I really must be made for this type of thing. Hiding bodies for thugs must be a calling.

I put my finished work into the cooler and make my way over to the Rhys look-alike. I pull the drawer out and look again at his face. He doesn't have many similarities once I'm in full blown comparison- mode– just enough to intrigue me.

He's wearing the same wife- beater tank- top and I find he has the same exact tattoo as Rhys. An eagle with wide spread wings, right across his chest. It must be some sort of insignia for their club, or whatever you call it.

I picture the quarter sized burn scar under the left wing, and can't help but think that he would make a fine substitution for what I need from Rhys. The thought seems to have hit the nail on the head; I feel that strong tingle between my legs that has only ever come from Rhys.

I trace the tattoo, running my finger across the full outline of it. I get lost in a sort of trance while my fingers work across his flesh, cool from the refrigerator.

The heat swells inside of me, hitting me deep inside my core. I can picture Rhys here right now; I can see all the things I want to see– need to see. I pull the scalpel from my pocket, cutting the fabric from his chest, opening it wide to display the rest of his tattoos. Although, very different from what Rhys has adorned, it still does the trick. The only thing missing is the hint of a scar under the wing.

I go to my purse, pulling a cigarette from the pack, and light it. I take a long satisfying pull from it and touch it to his chest, branding him with the mark of Rhys. I run my finger over it, and feel what it would be like to touch Rhys.

All I need now is something to enhance him. I go to the cupboard and find my hardening filler, mix the proper ratio and inject it into the underside of his cock, stretching it and massaging it to distribute the filler evenly throughout his shaft. The stroking motion of this cock adds to my excitement.

My mouth begins to water as I imagine my hand wrapped around Rhys. I have trouble getting the filler into the head of his cock and suddenly I find myself wrapping my lips around it and sucking hard in an effort to draw some up into the tip. It's so exhilarating I nearly get lost in it till I feel the compound start to harden against my tongue. This should effectively give him a hard and usable cock, it's fast acting and it should be done in under a minute. I watch as the solution swells, he is hung and thick, once it's full and standing at attention.

I give the taut cock a little squeeze to test its ability to handle what I have planned for it. It's firm and should be ready for me. I go first to the door and make sure to lock it, not wanting a repeat of what happened last time.

I peel my clothes off, leaving them scattered on the floor as I go. I can hardly wait to get him inside of me. I take it slow, lowering myself down on top of him inch by inch– and there are many inches.

I'm trying my hardest to take my time with him. To feel everything I crave. His cock is warm, heated by the activation of the mixture, and feels so good as it slides deep inside of me.

I hone in on the similarities of Rhys, picking out each inch that reminds me of him. And in no time it is Rhys I find under me. It's him I'm fucking, and it is the most dizzying feeling, capturing him like this in my mind. Once I get to that place, I lose control and have no choice but to submit. My pace goes from slow to frenzied within seconds.

Soon after, I come hard, shivering goosebumps across my flesh. I collapse on top of him, a sheen of sweat covers my tired body, and the contrast of my heat and his cool only amplifies the experience. It's a completely orgasmic feeling. A girl could really get used to this.

I climb off him and go get the furnace ready for him. I can't necessarily keep him, even if I'd very much like to. I send him into it with a little regret. Then I get dressed and do some of the cleaning that needs to be done for the evening.

five

I sleep better than I have in weeks.
Quenching a little of my obsessive need for
Rhys, through the use of his friend, really did
a number on my moral. The day flies by, and
just as I'm heading upstairs for the night,
Rhys walks in alone; I'm startled that I didn't
hear him before I saw him.

"Hey, pretty lady," he says, turning my
panties wet.

I don't have any idea why he would be
here tonight, and without a body for me to

handle. My thoughts run wild of what it could be; maybe he's here off the clock and hoping I'll be available for him.

Oh my god, if only.

I want it to be true so badly that I can taste it. Right on the tip of my tongue, the way I want to taste him. I lick my lips, as the flavor of him actually turns tangible. I salivate at the thought of him rolling his tongue around mine and fucking deep into my mouth, showing just how badly he needs to taste me, as well.

I step closer to him, his body calling to me, the magnetic pull I feel when around him is greater than gravity. The pull of him calling me nearer still, until I am mere inches from him, he doesn't step back and I take that as an invitation to climb up on the tips of my toes and reach for his mouth.

I don't feel it right away and have to open my eyes to find it. What I see though, crushes me; his face is twisted in repulsion. He puts his hands up and pushes me back by my shoulders, bringing us arms- length apart.

He holds my eyes with his, his face only slightly loosening and becoming more natural. "Listen, you're stunning, and we can still be tender to each other, but under no circumstances am I going to get anywhere near that hole of yours, I may be a lot of things, things that you think you like, and things that you have no idea about, but I'm not a man who follows after a dead guy. I will be making no concessions. It will be over my dead body that something like that will ever happen."

The words are harsh; they hit me in the pit of my soul. I can't hear anything else, the rush of blood is pumping hard, and taking away that sense. My vision blurs in rage. I never imagined this was a possibility, all the times I've thought about this, run it through my head, I never once thought the outcome could be anything other than us together, fucking like rabbits, ravaging each other. I can't wrap my head around this version. This fucked up version where he is not just as excited and eager for me. I feel duped, stupid, or both.

I am spitting mad, gritting my teeth hard enough to cause an ache. I don't realize the extent of what I'm capable of until I feel it. The scalpel tucked into my coat pocket, the cool metal feel of it in my fist.

I'm on him before he can react and stop me. My blade slicing right into his jugular, the arterial spray blinding me as it comes gushing out. I spit what gets in my mouth, but I still taste it, the tangy fluid dripping down my face, covering me in its warm wetness. He stumbles back clenching at his throat in an attempt to somehow save his blood from leaving his body. I push him down onto his back and sit on his chest, my knees pinning his arms beneath them.

I get close to his face, looking right in his knowing eyes and whisper, "as you wish."

I watch him die, no strength to even fight for his life. It flowed from him quicker than his blood left. I see in his eyes the horror that I am. He knows what I've done to him, he may even have some regret for being so mean, but it's too late now, nothing can bring him back from this.

And now he's all mine.

six

I get control of my heart rate as I stand and look at what I've done, what my impulsive reaction caused. I am both horrified and turned on. I'm so fucked up, he had me so twisted, so obsessed, that I couldn't handle those words, I couldn't fathom the possibility that he didn't want me just as much. How could my feelings be so strong for him and his not be the same for me? I suppose I could have been projecting my feelings for him onto him, manifesting it into reality. The thought hurts to my very core.

The loss is in the back of my mind, as the reality of having him available to me now, takes a leap to the forefront. I feel that tingle he gives me, deep between my legs. The butterflies in my tummy start dancing around, making me light- headed and excited.

I lower the table to floor height and heave his body on to it, undress and wash him. I need him looking as close to alive as I can get. I get lost in the process, his cock mostly, I touch it, feel the softness of it. Unless it was him putting his hands on me, I've never touched him, and now I have free reign to do with him all the things I have literally been dreaming of for all this time.

I push my finger into his mouth to feel his tongue, the piece of him I want with a desperation unparalleled by anything else in this world.

I need it.

I put my mouth to his, dipping my tongue into it, tasting him for the first time. His lips are soft, softer than I'd imagined they'd be. I suck his lip into my mouth and pull hard on it, biting a little to feel it between my teeth. I'm so hungry for him.

I slide my hands around his body, tracing all the detailed artwork and the muscle's divots along the way. He's still warm and soft, it's almost possible to imagine he's still alive. I lift his arm and put his hand on my chest, manipulating him to squeeze my tit. The feel of him touching me is overwhelming; it sends a rush between my legs. I make him squeeze harder.

The urge to have these fingers inside of me takes over, I pull my soaked panties off then bring his hand to my pussy, turn it upward, and push them inside of me. I want him to touch me everywhere; I want to feel him all over me. It doesn't even matter that he is not doing it on his own, it's still his hands touching me, even though I'm the one in control of them.

His thick fingers spread me wide and fill me up; I grind my hips and push him deeper, putting my own inside to guide his fingers to the spot that makes me so wet. My legs get weak, and I know I won't be able to stand for much longer. Regretfully, I pull his hand away from me.

I move to the tray with all my implements on it and take the suture kit over to him. I need that tongue, but without his muscles, it won't do me any good. I pull it out of his mouth and cut the underside to elongate it and make it usable. Then use a thread and needle to sew it to his lips, making it look like he's sticking it out. I taste it again, twirling mine around his. I can almost imagine all the words he's ever said to me in his beautiful accent, using this tongue to do so.

I take the rest of my clothes off and climb on him, pressing my body against the full length of his. I put a dab of lubricant on his tongue to wet it, then turn around and push my pussy right against it, grinding myself against him. I want his cock in my mouth and in this position; I simply lean over and suck it. I wish I could taste him, have him fill my mouth with come and really savor it, have him feed me.

I'm disappointed that it will never happen, but it doesn't stop me from sucking it into my mouth until my lips kiss his skin. He tastes so good. Feels so good inside of my mouth.

I make circles around the head with my tongue and imagine that he'd love that, that he would be so fucking hard for me, that I'd never be able to fit him inside my mouth from being so turned on by me.

I work my pussy up and down his mouth, sliding quicker as I feel that little tickle that tells me I'm ready. I can't stop myself, although I want to. I want it to last forever, but I can't pull away for even a second, it's been too long, and the tension has built up so much inside that little nub, that I need it gone.

A moan wells up from deep inside my throat and escapes around Rhys's cock, muffled only slightly by it, as I orgasm against his mouth. I keep myself pressed hard against him until the tremors stop.

My breathing slows and I can finally think straight, the constant state of arousal the last month was too much for my body, and the only thing that could satiate it, and help me be able to get back to the monotony of my life, was to have him. I just didn't know it would be instantaneous. I can feel all the tension fall away and the knots loosen around my body.

I lay my head against his thigh, pressing my mouth to it to put a few kisses around. I'm so grateful for the release, more than any other time in my life.

seven

I don't even realize that I had fallen asleep until I'm waking to the sound of the door crashing open. I can't remember why it should be frightening, why my heart pounds in my chest like a drum. Then it hits me– the flash of blood, the things that followed… me lying naked on a very dead Rhys.

Oh fuck.

I barely get my head turned in the direction of the door, when the loudest bang I've ever heard rings out in the tiny room. I never see what it was, but I feel right away that it hits me. And I know I'm dying, the bullet has gone through my neck, hard.

"That sick fucking bitch," I hear Leo say. The words are hard to hold on to. They leave my head a second later.

"She fucking killed him!" Thomas says.

There is a lot of blood pouring from me, so much I can't believe I'm still alive, my vision is hazy and I can't see anything individually, it's all just a blurry mess of colors. I can't breathe, I can't swallow to clear my throat. I can't hear them anymore. All I can do is lie here and wait, but I can't find a single regret here, as everything flashes by, I don't wish it had gone differently. I get to take my final breath while connected to Rhys. The last thing I do on this earth is turn my head and press it into the warmth of his skin. And there's never been a better, more complete feeling.

The End

Printed in Great Britain
by Amazon